ENZO the WONDERFISH

By Cathy Wilcox

TICKNOR & FIELDS Books for Young Readers
New York · 1994

For Andrew

First American edition 1994 published by
Ticknor & Fields Books for Young Readers
A Houghton Mifflin company, 215 Park Avenue South,
New York, New York 10003.

First published by Angus & Robertson,
an imprint of HarperCollins Publishers Pty Limited,
Sydney, Australia 1993.

Manufactured in the United States of America

Typography by David Saylor
The text of this book is set in 15 point Cheltenham Book
The illustrations are watercolor and pen and ink, reproduced in full color

HOR   10   9   8   7   6   5   4   3   2   1

Library of Congress Cataloging-in-Publication Data

Wilcox, Cathy.
Enzo the Wonderfish / by Cathy Wilcox.
p. cm.
Summary: A child who wants a pet is given a fish and vows to
train him to do wonderful tricks.
ISBN 0-395-68382-3
[1. Pets—Fiction. 2. Fishes—Fiction.] I. Title.
PZ7.W6453En 1994
[E]—dc20
93-11021   CIP   AC

I had always wanted a pet.
A pet, not quite as smart as me,
that I could feed and care for and pat.

I was the littlest.

It was always me
who was poked and prodded,
tickled and teased,
but sometimes I was cuddled.

Mom and Dad said,
"No more brothers and sisters."

That was fine with me—
if we could just get a pet.

First, I asked for a horse.
But Dad said, "Where would we keep it?"

Then, I begged for a dog.

"It's not fair to have a dog
when no one is home all day," said Mom.

"What about a cat?"

Dad scratched his whiskers.
"I think your sister's allergic," he said,
then sneaked away
without even telling me
what a *lergic* meant.

"A bird? They're cheap."

"No, I can't stand to see
a bird in a cage," said Mom,
and flew off in a huff.

"How about a rat?"
my brother asked, snickering.

But I thought one rat
in the family was enough.

I kept on trying,
but there were all sorts of reasons
why goats
and ducks
and guinea pigs
and mice
couldn't be my pets.

Then, on my seventh birthday,
my family shouted, "SURPRISE!"
and handed me my present in a bowl.

That was Enzo.
Cold and wet and goggle-eyed
and . . . my pet.

"There," said Dad,
"a fish is just as good as any other pet."

"You wait!" I told them all.
"I'll teach him to perform great feats!
He'll be Enzo the Great!
Enzo the Magnificent! Enzo . . . the Wonderfish!"

I didn't want Enzo to feel lonely,
so I put him on my shelf
next to my family of wooden dolls.

I put my lamp above him—
a wonderfish has to get used
to being in the spotlight.

I went to the library and took out a book for me and Enzo called *Training Your Pet.*

I looked for the section on
Tricks for Fish, but there wasn't one.
Somebody must have torn it out.

"Never mind," I told Enzo.

There were plenty of things to learn,
like *fetch* and *heel* and *stay*.

I found a very tiny stick
to throw for Enzo.

"Fetch, Enzo!"

The stick floated but
Enzo just swam around it.

"Get the ball, Enzo!"

Enzo showed no interest at all
in retrieving it.

I decided to try
something easier,
so I took Enzo for a walk.

The water slopped and splashed
along the sidewalk.

I don't know if fish get seasick,
but Enzo looked as though he was.
I took him home.

There were still so many tricks
for Enzo to learn,
but there was no point in moving too fast.
I'd take it step by step.

Maybe if I showed him how,
he could master
some simple commands.

"Sit," I said, sitting down
as fishily as I could.
Enzo kept swimming.

"Beg," I said,
showing him
how to hold
his fins.

Enzo kept swimming.

"Roll over!"   "Down!"   "Come!"   "Stay!"   "Play dead!"

I showed him
all the tricks
but it was no use.

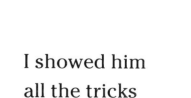

Enzo just wasn't interested.
All he wanted to do was swim
and blow bubbles
like some *ordinary* fish.

I needed a rest from training Enzo.
Maybe Enzo needed a rest, too.

I raced outside without even saying, "Stay!"

After dinner I went back
to my room and my shelf and the bowl
and my pet fish, Enzo.

ENZO!

I looked behind the books,
but Enzo wasn't there.

I looked inside the wooden dolls one by one,
but he wasn't there either.

I looked along the shelf,
and on my desk,
and on the floor,
but he wasn't anywhere.

The library book was open
to the page on leaping.

Enzo must have leapt.
But where?

He wasn't in my paintbrush holder
or in my ink bottle
or in my mug of crayons.

Then I found him,
floating in my teacup,
not moving at all.

"Mom! Dad! Everybody!
I think Enzo's dead."

Everyone came to look.

Dad fished Enzo out of the teacup,
and dropped him, *plop,* back in his bowl,
where he floated sideways.

"It's my fault," I said.
"I shouldn't have pushed him so hard."

"No, dear," said Mom, "don't blame yourself.
Fish sometimes jump."

And she cuddled me.

Just then, something moved in Enzo's bowl.
It was Enzo!

He was right-side up and swimming again!

Enzo flashed me a knowing look
that told me he'd just learned his second trick:

Playing dead!